Craig M'Nure

by

Shoo Rayner

Illustrated by Shoo Rayner

You do not need to read this page - just get on with the book!

First published in 2002 in Great Britain by
Barrington Stoke Ltd
10 Belford Terrace, Edinburgh EH4 3DQ

Printed by Polestar AUP Aberdeen Ltd

MEET THE AUTHOR AND ILLUSTRATOR - SHOO RAYNER

What are your favourite animals?
Cats – what else?

What is your favourite boy's name?
Max

What is your favourite girl's name?
I love all girls names!

What is your favourite food?
Cheese

What is your favourite music?
Prince

What is your favourite hobby?
Plumbing and plastering

What is your favourite website?
http://www.shoo-rayner.com

For Lindsey and Colin

Contents

Chapter 1
Guys from the Sky

I bet you saw that TV programme about me and my island and I bet you laughed like everyone else. Well, I can tell you that what they said was all lies! I am now writing this book so you will know what it's really like.

Craig M'nure's my name and manure's my game, as it says on the side of my tractor. I'm not ashamed to say that I make my living out of bird poo. In fact, I'm proud

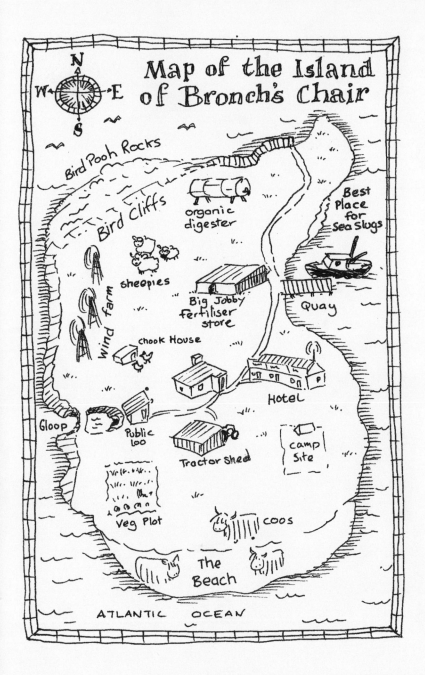

of what I do. I even managed to get the publishers to print this book on paper that's the same colour as puffin poo!

Let me start my story at the beginning.

I live on a tiny island called Bronch's Chair, in the middle of the Atlantic Ocean. I scrape bird poo off the rocks. I put the poo into bags and send it to my cousin in Scotland, who turns it into 'Big Jobby', the world's finest garden manure.

I'm just doing what my father did before me, and his father did before him. Once you've tasted a potato that's been grown in Big Jobby, you'll understand that what I do is not just a job, it's a vocation – it's my mission in life! I feel proud to have been chosen.

Not an awful lot happens on my island. Sometimes we get visitors, who come to study the amazing wildlife. They're usually

outdoor types who bring tents and look after themselves.

By the way, when I say we, I mean myself and my wee dog, Angus. I wouldn't want you to think I was a lonely, old fool who talked to himself!

Once in a while, something strange will happen on the island. I know it's in the middle of nowhere, but it's nearly on the way to somewhere, so you can never be sure what will appear over the horizon.

One day, from out of the sky, a helicopter appeared and landed in my yard. If there's one thing this island is famous for, it's wind, but the blast from the blades of that helicopter nearly blew the house down.

These big guys got out. They were wearing bright orange suits and helmets like they were aliens or something. Angus went barking mad!

The guys were from the phone company. The island has been used as a halfway staging post for the phone cable to the USA. This cable was laid across the Atlantic Ocean in 1952. We've had free phone calls ever since. I sometimes worry that they might bring me a phone bill one day!

It turned out that they wanted to lay a new cable across the ocean, a modern fibre-optic one. The information superhighway was coming right past my front door! The INTERNET was coming to Bronch's Chair.

The fibre-optic signal couldn't get across the ocean in one go, so they wanted to build a booster station on the island. It would take them a few months to do all the work, so they asked if they could build a hut that they could live in for a while.

Soon, an even bigger helicopter arrived with the hut hanging underneath it in

several parts. This was no garden shed. When it was put together, it was massive!

When all the work was finished and the cable had been laid, the men went home. The hut was left behind with the booster station in it. They said I could use the rest of the hut if I looked after the booster station for them.

The booster station was just a box that stood in the corner of one room. It didn't do much except flash lights on and off. But (and here's the best bit) it was connected to a computer with the fastest internet connection in the whole world, and I could use it for free!

I've never been afraid of hi-tech stuff, and I love playing with big boys' toys. So, it didn't take me long to get to grips with the internet.

Everything you need is there. If you don't know how to do something, there's either a website to explain it to you or someone you can email. People on the internet are very helpful.

Chapter 2
Website Madness

The winters are terribly cold and bleak on the island. Sometimes the wind blows so hard you can't stand up. The winter nights are long and dark. I was snowed up in my house for most of January. Poor Angus couldn't even get out for a pee! So I had plenty of time to build my Craig M'nure Website.

The day my website went live on the internet was a bit of a let-down. I thought something would happen right away, but nothing did. I had hoped the whole world would want to have a look at it. They didn't.

But the next day, I had my first email – it was from a Scotsman who lives in South America. He said my website made him feel like he was back home.

Then I had an email from a friend of his. Then I got emails from friends of his friends. Before long, I was getting more emails than I could answer, from people all around the world.

There is one website that tells you who has the most visited website on the internet. Mine was soon among the most popular, and newspapers began to write about me.

It wasn't long before I got an email from a TV station in London. They wanted to make a programme about me. They said there had been lots of programmes about people who had been left on islands to see how they survived.

Now they wanted to make a film about me, a real-life island survivor! All I had to do was carry on doing what I normally did every day and they would film me. They seemed to be really interested in my work.

Like I said before, I'm really proud of my work and I thought that a TV programme would be a chance to share my passion for poo with a wider world. Also, it sounded like a bit of fun, and they were paying me good money too!

They asked where they could stay on the island. I thought about the phone

company's hut – it had bunk-beds and a shower, that's four star heaven round here!

I'd already had the idea of renting the hut to visitors, so I told them they could stay at the *hotel*! They were going to pay me good money for that, too.

When spring came, I began getting ready for the TV crew's arrival. I painted a sign that said HOTEL above the door that led to the bunk-bed room. Over the middle door of the hut, where the phone company men had cooked and eaten their meals, I painted another sign that said DINING ROOM.

Over the door to the booster station room, I painted another sign that said CYBER CAFÉ. I made a kind of sofa out of old, wooden boxes I'd found on the beach, and rigged up a windmill on the roof that gave enough power to work the kettle. It took an hour to boil the water, but I didn't

want them to think I was still stuck in the twentieth century!

The big day arrived. My wee dog Angus and I stood on the headland staring out to sea. A tiny dot appeared on the horizon. It was my cousin Duggie bringing the TV crew to the island on his boat.

There were two of them. They were clearly not sailors! When they arrived at the jetty, their faces were the colour of puffin poo.

I thought that it was probably normal for people who lived in London and never got any fresh air to look like that. Well, you do hear such stories about the place! But Duggie told me they had started off quite fit and healthy but had been throwing up over the side of his boat ever since they left the mainland.

Angus took an instant dislike to them. He stood at the water's edge and growled at them. By the look on his face, I knew he'd bite their ankles if he could.

Duggie and I helped the two of them off the boat and laid them down on some sacks in my trailer. They groaned like a couple of stranded whales and that's just what they looked like, too!

****

I drove the tractor carefully up to the hotel and they wailed and grunted every time I went over a wee bit of a bump.

I showed them their rooms. When I offered them some peppermint tea they turned a sort of green colour and buried themselves beneath the covers. What strange people, peppermint tea sorts out my guts as fast as lightning.

Duggie and I unloaded their cases and all the stores I'd asked him to bring.

They must have been really ill. We didn't see them again until the next day. Duggie and I knocked on the hotel door to see if they were ready for breakfast.

"Good morning!" I said. "I've got some nice fish, fried herrings, I've got seaweed bread, or I could see if the hens have laid some eggs today, or I could go and milk one

of the coos if you'd just like breakfast cereal."

They turned that weird puffin poo colour again!

"Maybe a wee bit of porridge, then?" I suggested.

They managed to eat some porridge. They complained about it being salty though. They said they liked sugar on their porridge – have you ever heard of such a thing?

While we ate, Duggie told them that the tide was coming up fast and it was time for him to go back to the mainland. If they wanted to go with him, this was their last chance to leave the island until he returned for them in a week.

They smiled a lot and said, "Thank you, but we've come to do a job and we'll finish what we've started."

They stayed.

Chapter 3
The Gloop

Their names were Alice and Simon. When they finally came out of the hotel the next morning, they were looking a lot better.

It was a beautiful summer's day but they were wrapped up in bright red, padded jackets like it was winter.

"Is it always this cold?" Simon asked.

I looked around me. The sun was shining. A warm, gentle breeze was blowing from the south. "Cold?" I replied. "This is a heatwave!"

They had found the shower room but said they couldn't find the bathroom. It took a little while before I understood what they meant, and then I laughed.

"Oh, you mean the lavvy!" Then I had to explain about the toilets on the island. "The island is solid rock, so we can't have any drains here. I've an earth closet at my place – it's just a hole in the ground, but I think you'd rather go to the public lavvy. It's up at The Gloop. Follow the path and mind the coos."

"What's The Gloop, Craig?" Simon asked.

"Simon, I'm in a hurry," interrupted Alice. "Tell it to the camera later."

I watched them pick their way along the path. Simon trod in something and slipped. He swore loudly.

"Oh, and watch out for the coo poo!" I yelled.

When they returned, they had weird smiles fixed on their faces.

Alice got her camera out, while Simon explained how we were going to film the programme.

"What we want is to show your daily life here just as it is. We find it's best if you pretend that we aren't here. Just do what you would normally do, and we'll follow you around. If I ask you a question, don't talk to

me, talk to the camera as if it's your best friend."

A little red light twinkled on Alice's camera and the filming began. "Action!" she called.

Simon smiled through gritted teeth. "Craig," he asked, "would you mind talking to the camera and telling us what a coo is, and what exactly is a gloop?"

Well, that was easy.

"A coo is an island cow," I said. "I've a herd of twenty that live mostly on the beach. Their favourite food is seaweed which makes their poo amazingly rich and brilliant for garden manure.

"I put the coo-pats into bags and dry them out. On really cold days, I burn them

on the fire. Once they get crackling, my wee
house is soon nice and warm and toasty.

"The Gloop is the natural wonder of the
island," I went on to tell them. "It's a tunnel
that drops down into the roof of a cave. It can
be found on top of the western cliffs.

"At the bottom of the cliff, on the
seashore, is a large, deep cave. At high tide,
when the sea is rough and the wind is in
the west, the waves blast through this cave
and shoot up out of The Gloop like a rocket.

"It's over The Gloop's hole that I built
the public lavvy. It's quite a drop down into
the cave, but it's all right if you've got
something to read and you don't look down.

"The tide washes the cave out twice a
day so it's very clean. In fact, it beats the

drains on the mainland any day. But you'll need to watch out and stand clear when the wind is blowing hard from the west!"

Chapter 4
Lights, Camera, Action!

Simon and Alice were not happy.

I wasn't happy either. They followed me around all day, like a pair of stupid puppies.

They didn't know anything. They asked stupid questions all the time. If they weren't asking stupid questions, they were complaining about something or other.

They complained that I didn't have fluffy, white bread. (I've always made my own wholemeal bread. It helps to keep my insides in order.)

They complained that there wasn't any soft toilet paper. (What's toilet paper?)

They couldn't sleep because the sun hardly went down, and they couldn't stand the smell of bird poo so they wore scarves across their noses. (What smell of bird poo? I can't smell anything!)

If they weren't complaining, they were saying nothing at all – just hiding behind that twinkling red light on the camera. They were filming all the time.

They would turn their backs to me and they would huddle together to plot. They said they were planning what to film next, but I knew they were plotting against me!

They were stuck on my island until Duggie returned and there was no way off.

So I just went about my daily business and they followed me and filmed me with the camera.

Chapter 5
The B52s

Every year, millions of birds come back to the island to lay their eggs. Each pair returns to the same old nest. For the last ten years, the same pair of herring gulls have nested on the roof of my house.

I call them the B52s after the American Airforce bomber! Every year, the B52s come back to nest just above my front door. Every day, Mr B52 waits for me to come out of the house so that he can poo on my head.

Mrs B52 sits on the nest and cackles. Very funny, it is not!

Well, glory be, this year the B52s felt like a bit of a change and decided that Simon and Alice were far more interesting targets to aim at. The B52s moved their nest to the hotel roof and I had a poo-free year.

Whenever Simon and Alice poked their heads out of the hotel, old Mr B52 was waiting for them! Splat! He was a master bomber and never missed. I had an idea that it was probably their fancy, red padded jackets that had caught his eye.

"Duck down!" I exclaimed.

Simon fell to his knees and covered his head with his clipboard.

"No!" I laughed. "Not duck down like that! It's the *duck down* in your padded

jackets that annoys them. Mr B52 must think you're a rival birdie after his nest!"

Simon and Alice had to choose either to wear their jackets, all covered in poo, or to freeze. I still couldn't believe they were cold, after all, we were having a heatwave!

As I said at the beginning, M'nure's my name and manure's my game. I hadn't realised how much of my life was involved with poo until I had to spend each day talking about it to the camera.

During the long summer days, while the birds are fixing up their nests and feeding their young, there's a lot of poo to be scraped up.

There's a game I like to play while I collect up the coo poo. I call it tossing the coo poo. I choose a place to pile them up and mark it with a stick. Then I throw the

coo poos at the target. When they're really dry, they fly like frisbees.

I reckon I'd get a gold medal if they did it in the Olympics! Angus likes to try and catch them as they fly through the air.

"Oh! That's so sweet!" yelled Alice. "Do you think you could throw one in this direction so I can film Angus catching it?"

I chose a chunky one that Angus would find easy to grab hold of, and tossed it towards where Alice was filming. "Angus," I called, "catch it, boy!"

As Angus leaped in the air, a gust of wind lifted it out of his jaws and whisked it splat, in the middle of Alice's face. It was crispy on the top but still quite soggy underneath. It didn't hurt, but Alice swore that I'd aimed it at her. I'm good, but not that good!

Oh, I've not told you about the Sheepies. Sheepies are special to the island. You'll not find them anywhere else. They're not really much use, but their poo does feed the loofah grass on the island and that's what keeps it looking so nice and green. I tried to explain that you shouldn't stand behind them.

"What's the matter?" Simon asked. "Do Sheepies kick?"

We were standing in the middle of a flock of them. "No, they don't kick," I said. "But when Sheepies poo, they shoot tiny, little pellets out with such force, they can hit a target 30 metres away. Be careful, they'll knock your hat off!"

Then, out of the corner of my eye, I saw one of their tails lift up. I yelled out, "Simon, duck!"

"Where?" Simon said.

The fool was looking in the sky for ducks.

It was too late. He was knocked to the ground by rapid machine-gun fire. His nice, red jacket was covered in black spots where he had been hit. He looked like a giant ladybird. Those stains will never come out!

I think I can safely say that Simon and Alice came into contact with most of the exotic bird life on the island.

The Pee Wee is a bird that got its name because it likes to wee on your head. Alice used up all her shampoo and still couldn't get rid of the smell.

Then there's a kind of gull that only lives on Bronch's Chair. It pukes up food for its young. It also spits a jet of vomit at

anyone who comes too close. It's revolting stuff that can strip paint off a door. It took the lovely, shiny, silver finish off Alice's camera!

Chapter 6
Curry Surprise!

Once or twice we nearly had a punch-up and it was clear that Simon and Alice blamed me for everything that had happened to them. But they managed to survive until Duggie came back.

All week they had been complaining about the food I cooked for them. The day before they left, I overheard Simon telling Alice that he couldn't wait to get back to

London so he could go out for a slap-up curry.

"Oh, you like curry, do you?" I asked. "I can cook curry! Seeing as it's your last night on the island, we can make a bit of a party of it, to show there are no hard feelings." I didn't want them to go home in a bad mood with me.

I spent the whole afternoon working like a slave to prepare a huge, steaming pile of curry. It was my own special recipe. There's nothing quite like it to clear out your inner tubes.

"This is great!" Simon exclaimed. "You should open a restaurant in London and sell this stuff. What's in it?"

Seeing how sensitive they were about their food, I thought it would be better if they didn't know about the island's special

treat. Sea slugs are very tasty but they don't look too pretty until they're cooked. Then they look a bit like chicken.

"Oh, it's the very best seafood that the island has to offer!" I said and smiled sweetly.

They seemed to be really grateful that I'd made such an effort and soon we were

laughing and joking about all the ups and downs of their week-long stay.

Although I say it myself, it was an excellent curry. Simon had two helpings!

I left them early, so they could get a good night's sleep before their journey home the next day.

As I left the hotel, I looked up at the sky and saw dark clouds. I licked a finger and held it in the air to get a feel for the bad weather that I knew was moving in.

"There's a fair old gale brewing up from the west," I called out to them, as I closed the door behind me.

It was a humdinger of a storm. Angus, as usual, slept through it. Then, right in the middle of the storm, as the lightning flashed and sheets of rain lashed against

the windows, Angus raised his head and growled.

I know all his little growls, and this one meant that Simon was out and about.

I looked through the window and saw the beam of Simon's torch sway to and fro, as he battled his way to The Gloop.

This was not the night to need the lavvy. I put my waterproofs on and battled my way to The Gloop.

It was the worst storm the island has seen since 1972. I tried calling out to Simon, but my voice flew away on the wind.

I fought my way to the lavvy but I was too late. Simon was already inside. With the wind howling all around me, I could still hear him groaning. He must have eaten too

much curry. (I told you it cleared out the inner tubes.)

I peered out to sea. The rain was battering my face. Then suddenly, a monstrous wave loomed out of the darkness. It was heading for the cliffs and the cave down below. I banged on the door and shouted at the top of my voice, "Simon, you've got to get out now!"

"Urrgh!" was the only reply.

The wave crashed into the cliff, filling the cave with water. There was only one way for it to go.

I heard the water rush up the tunnel as it looked for a way out. With an almighty "Glooooop!" a fountain of water blasted out of the roof of the lavvy. Surfing on top of it, with his trousers round his ankles was Simon.

I've never seen anyone look so surprised.

Chapter 7
Fame at Last

Simon and Alice didn't come to breakfast the next day. They took all their things down to the jetty and waited for Duggie to come and get them. They didn't even say goodbye.

I could have told them there was a very high tide expected that day. I couldn't be bothered – I'd had enough of them, too. Angus and I watched as the water surged

over the jetty and swept away their fancy cases.

Luckily, the tide was coming in so the cases were washed ashore in the seaweed beds. Simon got very wet rescuing them. He slipped on something and fell, headfirst, into a rockpool.

"That'll be a sea slug," I told Angus. "They're very slippery if you tread on them!"

At last, Duggie's boat arrived to take them home. Simon and Alice couldn't get their things on board fast enough.

As the engine started up, I heard Simon's voice drift across the waves. "We're free! We're safe. We're going home at last."

He hadn't reckoned on the B52s. With the sun behind them, the gulls swooped down on a final bombing run to leave Simon and Alice a present to remember them by.

The sea air turned blue with Simon's curses.

They took a lot of film back to London with them.

That's where they had their revenge on me. We never used to get the TV out here, but now there's the satellite I get to see everything.

They made a right fool out of me.

The programme showed me happily at my work talking about poo like it was my whole life. I sounded like a babbling idiot! I can't help it! If you work with something every day, you get to be an expert.

But they made it look like I was obsessed with poo even though I've got lots of other interests – like wind power for example. That's where all my electricity comes from.

I had hoped that people would see the programme and would want to come and stay at my hotel.

When I saw the programme, Simon and Alice had made it look as if it was just an old hut. *No-one would want to come and stay on the island the way they showed it,* I thought.

Well. I got so angry, I sat right down and wrote this book to get my side of the story straight. I got it all off my chest and then I felt a whole lot better.

An awful lot of people watched that programme and after it was shown on TV, my website became the most popular in the world and I got into the record books.

So many people wanted to come and visit the island and stay at the hotel after they saw the film and visited my website,

www.shoo-rayner.com. The hotel is booked up for the next three years!

Such interesting people want to come to stay. Gas engineers, manure salesmen, compost experts and others who come in search of the simple life and good, fresh island cooking.

They all love my curry and they all go away with special hats to remind them of the island. The hats have 'I survived the B52s' printed on them.

So the island of Bronch's Chair is famous now. It just goes to show that the old saying is true – 'it's an ill wind that brings no-one any good!'

Who is Barrington Stoke?

Barrington Stoke was a famous and much-loved story-teller. He travelled from village to village carrying a lantern to light his way. He arrived as it grew dark and when the young boys and girls of the village saw the glow of his lantern, they hurried to the central meeting place. They were full of excitement and expectation, for his stories were always wonderful.

Then Barrington Stoke set down his lantern. In the flickering light the listeners were enthralled by his tales of adventure, horror and mystery. He knew exactly what they liked best and he loved telling a good story. And another. And then another. When the lantern burned low and dawn was nearly breaking, he slipped away. He was gone by morning, only to appear the next day in some other village to tell the next story.

Barrington Stoke would like to thank all its readers for commenting on the manuscript before publication and in particular:

Grace Alexandra Allan
Subat Bashir
Luke Bennett
Michelle Cuthbertson
Kaylee Furber
Stuart Gillespie
Suzanne Graham
Matthew Hill
Robin Hoque
Chloe Horsfield
Sam Hudson
Justine Hughes
Sarah Hunter
Mehvish Hussain
Emma Jesse

Jade Nicolle Jones
Huma Khaliq
Veronica Lewis
Saddaf Mahmood
Sharina Munroe
Maggie Neill
Charelle Nichols
Sean Nixon
Nicholas Ross
Sommia Shaheer
Christopher Shrubsole
Angela Smith
Hayley Spittles
Amy Stewart
Robbie Tamplin
Aliyah Yousuf

Become a Consultant!

Would you like to give us feedback on our titles before they are published? Contact us at the address or website below – we'd love to hear from you!

Barrington Stoke, 10 Belford Terrace, Edinburgh EH4 3DQ
Tel: 0131 315 4933 Fax: 0131 315 4934
E-mail: info@barringtonstoke.co.uk
Website: www.barringtonstoke.co.uk

If you loved this story, why don't you read...

Young Dracula

by Michael Lawrence

Have you ever felt like you don't belong? Some day, Wilfred will become Count Dracula - the greatest, most feared vampire of them all. But his father, the old Count, doesn't think Wilfred is up to the job. He thinks Wilfred is a wimpire! Can Wilfred show his father what he is really made of?

You can order this book directly from:
Macmillan Distribution Ltd, Brunel Road, Houndmills,
Basingstoke, Hampshire RG21 6XS
Tel: 01256 302699